Love and Something Else

Love and
Something Else
A Twisted Tale of Life

ANANYA BHANJA CHAUDHURI

PARTRIDGE
A Penguin Random House Company

To order additional copies of this book, contact
Partridge India
000 800 10062 62
orders.india@partridgepublishing.com

www.partridgepublishing.com/india

Contents

This is the first book by the author-

Ananya Bhanja Chaudhuri

To my parents

"Yeh toh sirf agas hay, suruwad hai safar ka. Mein nehi koi yodhdha, lekhin meri kalam hi aujaar hain"

- Ananya Bhanja Chaudhuri

Acknowledgements

Thank you readers and friends for picking up my first book: Love and Something Else. Here's thanking all those who helped me with this book.

When one writes a book, indeed it's you who is doing the actual writing, but if certain people aren't there throughout your writing process, it would have been impossible on your part to go ahead with the book.

My Family members especially my mother, who always inspired me to take up the pen and unfold my thoughts in the notebook. She often freed me from the daily chores and advised to concentrate on my writing. My father made all the arrangements for writing even missed his favourite TV shows so that I am in peace of mind while working on it. Also thank my brother and his family for believing in my work and constantly supporting me all along.

I want to thank all my colleagues who pushed me to go ahead with the publication procedure, as they too wanted to see my book placed in the shelves of the nearest book stores more than I did. I also thank the CEO or my organization for being an absolute inspiration with the thought that "believe in you and go ahead with it, always be hungry for more".

I sincerely thank Partridge India to come up with their finest publication services when I was feeling disappointing with the stringent procedure. They made it so easy and smooth that I went ahead with them and promising myself to do all the future publishing with them only.

Preface

$\mathcal{L}$ove is an absolute necessity of our survival. As humans it's the bonding, the attachment that keeps us going. We name it as love. When I had started writing I had no clue about this. I was casually writing short stories based on pure mushy mushy love between a boy and a girl.

And then one day I met a friend who was going through a tough time with her husband because of the presence of a third person in the relationship. Their entire life had gone upside down. I took a lesson and said- enough is enough. If a relationship can go on like that even being through all the drama of heartbreaks and mistrust, so such stories must be heard.

I went ahead and questioned my friends and colleagues and found out outstanding facts about relationships which I had no idea before. Then when I started working of it the story came back to me and asked myself what should and where should it redirect after the end of each chapter.

I story isn't simply about ups and downs in relationships. It's an inspiration in itself giving people a hope to go ahead even after things seem to have gone worse. This story, I believed must be heard by everyone. All along you will go through different emotional upheavals and the end will take to where your heart will fill with absolute satisfaction that love ultimately survived for good.

Don't let loved ones leaving you forever. Take time and make necessary adjustment if not compromise for your loved ones.

This is a story of people finding love, losing it and then going an extra mile to get it back. Well, what more, read the book to know the rest of it.

1

MY PERFECT WORLD

'*Hi* Reva!' No no… 'Hiiiiii Di! I misssseed you soooo much, love you so much.'

I repeated in my head. Then some emotional hugs and embracing and then again, 'Oh! Li'l Guddi is all grown up!' It went on and on.

I don't remember how long I have been rehearsing this in front of the mirror. But am sure I stayed long enough in the washroom that made Mohan knock at the door saying, "Are you all right in there?"

I shouted back, "Sure! Just a minute, sweetheart."

Yup! That's my sweetheart, *kuchiku, mistishona*[1], Mohanshona that's my husband. I wonder was he really worried or was it just that he wanted to make love for

---

[1]   Endearing term

the last time before I left for Kolkata tomorrow. I said to myself Ah! This is my life, my perfect life (with correction)!

For a fraction of a second I stood there hands stretched wide open in the air. Soon I realized I was going nuts myself. I felt sad at that moment to leave Mohan alone for such a long time. I came out to check what he was doing. He was already asleep with a Chetan Bhagat book open on his chest. I slowly walked towards him, took off the book and kissed his forehead. I was about to turn around when he pulled my right hand pleading, "Don't go."

The innocence with which he spoke, reminded me of the *Kuch Kuch Hota Hai*[2] dialogue- *Tusi ja rahe ho?Tusi na jao*[3].

I smiled and said, "S-h-o-n-a."

Mohan wide awake pleaded, "Don't lie, I hate you."

Was he about to cry, I was kind of amused and did enjoy to some extent. But his face was pale; I tell you men don't look good when they cry. But perhaps the only exception is Aamir Khan, the actor who looks good in every mood. It was in one of the episodes of *Satyameva Jayate*[4]when I saw him crying. It made me fall in love with him watching the show sitting beside my husband. Oh! Did I say 'love'? Later that day, I asked myself whether it was right for a married woman to even think like that. Correction! A happily married woman with a loving husband! But then Aamir is a national icon, so it's not wrong to fall for him. Even mom loved Swami Vivekananda, though she never mentioned

---

[2]   A Bollywood film
[3]   You are leaving? Please don't go
[4]   A popular TV show hosted by Aamir Khan

it, but her immense interest to learn all about him. This is my defense whenever I do something irrational. I compare with something mom did, not because I love her but mostly because she was so perfect in so many ways, that I put forward her action to legalize my action! I wanted to carry the tradition of being perfect. Though, I hated it whenever Revathi, my elder sister, called me a 'Good Girl'.

Even Guddi calls me by that name, like 'hey good girl, *mashi*⁵shona'.

My hubby got paler until I stretched my arms to hug him,"I Love You."

"I love you more."

I contradicted,"No. I love you most."

"Then prove it to me".

"How?" (Knowing where he was going with it).

"Make me a promise, you will call me every night and we will talk till we fall asleep, like the good old days."

All my enthusiasm fell flat. Just talk? Are we kids, why not a romantic video chat?

I smiled, "Promise," and stretched my hand.

He then kissed my hand. I surely was in the mood; c'mon this is our last night together. But, boy! Was he slow? I grabbed his hand and pulled him towards me. Then the obvious happened. I may not go into details, just that he cried all through.

I woke up early next morning to find the breakfast ready and served.

Mohan, "Good Morning Honey."

---

⁵ Mother's sister

He was looking unusually good. I mean handsome. Was it the effect of last night's venture or was he trying to hide his real feelings? I know he is terribly upset with my decision to attend Guddi's wedding in Kolkata without him. He can't go because he has to work his ass off to make through the promotion. He was avoiding any eye contact, I noticed that. I got hold of his hand when he was about to get the phone which was ringing. He slowly sat down on the bed and we stared at each other with empty eyes, while the phone kept ringing in the background, outweighed by the gravity of the situation. We startled when it stopped ringing. We said in unison, "Oh no!"

Mohan checked the CLI attached to the landline and smiled, "Oh! Don't worry, it was from your home, everyone must be excited to know when you are arriving."

I hurried towards the phone to ring back. And I heard someone screaming from the other end.

Guddi "mashi, tell me when are you coming. I will personally pick up the good girl from the airport and I will have a surprise for you." I was about to get mad at her address but then did she say something or did I hear it wrong? So I babbled," Did you just say 'surprise'?"

Guddi was taken aback as if she had offended me somehow,"Yes, I'm afraid I said so."

"Oh Guddi, I love surprises," I shouted.

Then we spoke for a while mostly what we will do after I reach Kolkata. How we would roam around aimlessly here and there, watch movies and eat *fuchka*[6] and all sorts

---

[6]   Roadside snack that is tangy and spicy

4

of junk that I missed so much. At the Bengaluru Airport the usual cliché dialogue between husband and wife continued…'I will miss you', 'please come back soon' and 'try to keep the promise'.

I showed thumbs up and entered through the gate. I don't know how long he waited there, must have been pretty long. I was feeling really bad to leave him back this way that too for fifteen days! But do I have a choice?

2

THE LONGEST JOURNEY

I was about to board the plane when Guddi called again, "Last minute change of plan mashi."

"What? Are you calling off the wedding?"

It was supposed to be a funny comment. But at that moment I sensed I might have upset her a bit.

"M-a-s-h-i you are something! Hahaha."

Her laughter was a relief, "Tell me then what change."

"Instead of me, Ryan —my fiancé will be picking you up from the airport."

I was totally under shock, how would I recognize him?

And then something strikes me and I crack another joke to make it sound easier, "What if I run away with him?" I laughed out loud.

Guddi chided, "C'mon mashi, good girl mashi, he is a good boy, you will like him. He will be your perfect escort up to home."

I said, "Ok" and hung up.

But in the whole two and half hour journey I panicked for no reason. I recalled that Guddi had once said that he was French guy and hardly been in India for long. As I was approaching the conveyer belt, I felt happy to be in my hometown.

As I was about to step out, I felt my eyes welling up but then I saw a small mass of people walking in my direction with garlands in their hands. I thought it could be for some popular cricketer or film star. So I swayed my way carefully to the exit pushing my luggage cart, which was quite heavy with two trolley bags and a huge purse. My eyes scanned through the people waiting there. But there was no sign of a white boy, rather a sardarji[7] trying to pull my baggage from my hand saying, "Madamji first time Kolkata, *tusi mere saath ayoji.*[8]"

"Oh no… leave it baba," I said desperate to estrange.

Guddi suddenly appeared like an angel to rescue me from the hassle, "M-a-s-h-i!"

She stretched her arms to hug. I retreated, "*Chal jhuti*[9]!"

Guddi smiled, "Come with me there is a surprise for you."

---

[7]   A man from Punjab
[8]   You come with me
[9]   You liar

I quickly walked towards the car standing outside and found everyone from Reva, *Jiju*[10], Dad and even poor Ryan gazing in awe. Then Guddi flung her hands in the air, "Surprise!!"

I put up a fake smile pretending to be happy to see them all. Then the routine hugging and embracing and little niceties with much perfection, seemed as if they too were practicing for the moment.

Reva exclaimed,"Lathi you look all the same."

I don't know why people say this every time you meet them. Isn't it the nicest way of saying you are looking 'old'? I laughed as if I was amused by the remark. They too joined it like a chorus until the security people asked us to clear the space. But then there was the prospect of traveling in the same car with Dad. I felt so suffocated, but then much to my relief Reva sitting next to Dad said, "You don't have to get in sweetie, Guddi hasa real surprise in store for you."

They drove off and we started walking towards the parking lot, "Wait here mashi."

Then again there was another round of surprise. She had brought the scooty for me. Now that is a surprise. Guddi knew my love for the scooty. So she said, "Like our good old days mashi, let's drive and glide."

I flung myself on the back seat, "Don't expect me to drive this thing."

---

[10]   Brother-in-law

Guddi started laughing as if I was cracking another joke,"Ok mashi, then sing with me, *aaj mein upar, asma niche, aaj mein ageh, jamana hai peche*[11], gao[12]na mashi-i-i-i."

The approximate time taken from DumDum Airport to our home in Baguiati is twenty minutes or so. But Guddi being in one of her mischievous moods took a longer route via Jessore road. At first I grabbed her tightly across the waist but soon I got into the mood too. It was fourth of January, the winter added to our delight. I un-clutched my hair so that the wind can play through them like a sitarist's fingers on the strings. All my happy memories were unfolding in front of me as Guddi kept on singing. Yes the three girls, whom the university students referred as 'Asma Girls' were making their first performance in the campus. "Oh those days, the best days of my life," I said to myself. I came to my senses when the bike suddenly stopped with a jerk at a crossing. Guddi asked half turning her head, "Did you ever have an adventure mashi?"

Surely I hated this interruption on my flashback. Then I thoughtfully replied, "Guddi if your idea of having an adventure is to break the traffic rules, then I am surely not into it."

She laughed out loud, "Oh good mashi, I didn't mean that. I said it just casually."

"It's never casual with you. You surely are up to something," I said.

---

11   Today I'm on high, the sky is below, today I'm ahead, time is left behind

12   Sing

"Did you see all the hotels with bars all along the road? I have an idea."

I warned, "Please Guddi, enough of this. I am too tired, I badly need some rest."

"I was just making an innocent query, you seem so disturbed," pouted Guddi.

Once home, I had to spill out the real problem bothering me for some time, "Do I have to stay at home? Why don't I stay at the guesthouse you arranged for the relatives?"

Guddi interrupted, "Those are for outsiders, plus we will have all the fun together, think about it. The 24x7 fun station just at your beck and call!!"

When we arrived home, we found Ryan standing outside, looking quite worried."What took you so long?"

"We took the long route. You see mashi arrived after such a long time, so much had changed, she insisted on catching up," smiled Guddi.

She winked at me. I winked back as if it was a secret pact. Then they kissed each other in front of me embarrassing me no end. I was apprehensive that Ryan will do the same with me. Then I see him walking towards me in slow motion. Ok ok … the motion was my imagination. But he bends to touch my feet to my utter relief. I bless him like any elderly in-law, "God bless you dear."

I saw Guddi laughing, "He never misses a chance to impress his in-laws. That's my man."

I smiled, even though I felt it was quite a scene.

Then we moved towards our flat on the third floor. We chose the stairs because it was Guddi's idea of having fun. C'mon they are still kids. Ryan had by then put his hand across Guddi's shoulder. And they were laughing and kissing as we walked ahead. I wondered that he must be a good kisser. As we reached the third floor Guddi knocked the door three times. Reva flung open the door shouting, "Oh Renu, have you come?"

Then she gazed at us for a while and laughed at her own mistake, "Come in you all. I thought it was Renu."

I know all about Renu because Reva talks about her all the time. She is the housemaid, a much sought after lady I must say; much in demand, probably that's why she makes only special appearances. She needs rest, money, less work all at the same time.

3

LANDING ON THE WRONG FOOT

I was all settled in the room, my room. I spent twenty seven years of my life in this room. I shared it with Mom. I took a deep breath – "I miss you Mom."

"Mom is no more with us," dad had said, when he called up that winter night. I know I could not reach here in time mainly because the weather was unpleasant and all flights were delayed. When I reached home from Bengaluru they had already taken her for cremation.

I said to myself –"His face disgusts me. Why didn't he wait for me? Is it because I was a girl who had nothing to do with the rituals or just that he never thought of me as worthy as Reva?" I could never forgive him for what he did to me, yes I hate my Dad. It may not come as a shock to many youngsters who too have similar feelings for their parents. But mine had some genuine reasons. He always made disparity between Reva and me. First and foremost, he chose a bad name for me - Lathika. Chiii…, that sounds so bad compared to Revathi Sen.

Next, once when I was playing hide-and-seek with Reva behind the door, which Dad knew quite well, he banged the door on my face and I had a bad cut on the forehead that I have to carry all my life.

Third reason, I was twelve years old when I got my first love letter from an elderly boy in our locality. Reva somehow sneaked through my bag and handed over the letter to Dad. It was not enough that he rebuked me so badly; he tore the letter to pieces in front of me.

Fourth reason, he always praised Reva for choosing engineering as her profession, while demeaning me in front of guests, "Here comes our wannabe journalist, please clap."

Fifth reason, then Reva married a Nepali guy, which he approved of instantly, just because he was an IIT[13] graduate. And here I was doomed for an arranged marriage, as I failed all his expectations.

I could go on and on with the list. But I was interrupted by Guddi who was obviously too excited with the wedding preparations going on. She wanted to discuss some details, the final checklist I guess. I assured to join her in a minute but before that I would like to have a quick chat with

---

[13]   Indian Institute of Technology- premier engineering college

'*Mesho*[14]'. She left with a smile and a warning, "Don't be naughty!"

It was seven-thirty in the evening; I knew Mohan would be still in office. I checked my mail and found him in 'idle' status, yet I 'pinged' him so that he could reply once he opens the page. I went ahead and opened another webpage and typed www.flipkart.com.

I wanted to check the list of best sellers available. Then something crossed my mind- soon my book will be available for sale out here, I was ecstatic when Guddi came rushing back, "Snacks time, snacks time!"

I said, "No, not now shona."

"Come on, I will show you something."

She almost dragged me to the dining table. "See I made these *aloo paranthas*[15] myself."

"What? *Parantha*s, at this hour? So are we skipping dinner?"

"No, you will digest it all by then, we will have dinner at eleven-thirty," pacified a smiling Reva.

So we all sat around the table in a strange orderly manner. Girls on one side the boys on the other. Guddi was sitting between me and Reva, as if we will feed her like we used to when she was a kid. Opposite Guddi sat Ryan, I wonder why was he always around, isn't it customary not to see the bride before the wedding? I turned my face to check if Dad was coming. He came a little later but sat on the adjacent sofa surfing the TV. Reva probably saw me

---

[14]   Mother's sister's husband
[15]   Handmade pan fried flatbread with potato stuffing

watching Dad and expecting some sympathy from me, said, "He isn't eating well, he seems so unhappy all the time."

I nodded and gave an expression of empathy. Suddenly I felt something on my feet; a strange feeling of something going up and down, it could be an insect but then I realized it was Ryan, the weirdo. I knew it from the very first time I laid my eyes on him; he was a pervert, a damn pervert. Then I saw him smiling mischievously at Guddi. This brought my heart back to its place. By then Guddi was shouting, "Hey *dadu*[16]'Star Ananda' channel please. Mashi this is Arvind Singh giving his speech against violence inflicted upon women. He is our hero."

She went on, "He was a very popular quiz master, now a member of parliament. But he dares to speak against the ruling party, the party he belongs to. They may expel him someday, but he is a risk taker."

I added smiling; "Now that is what I call stepping on the wrong foot."

I looked at Ryan and repeated, "Wrong foot Ryan, you understand?"

He got my hint and shifted his foot away, embarrassed and sat with composure like a disciplined child in front of guests after being chided.

Guddi asked again, "Mashi I heard he did his masters in Political Science, that too from CU[17]. Haven't you heard of him?"

---

[16]   Grandfather
[17]   Calcutta University

I kept my same indifferent look and replied, "No never."

We all consumed the tasty paranthas and discussed about decorations, clothing, guest list, more clothing, food items, and then came the interesting topic of how Guddi and Ryan found each other at the Academy of Fine Arts, due to their similar taste in Arts, how they had instantly fallen for each other and on and on.

Guddi was telling her big plan of decorating the room of her would be in-laws with flowers. To them it would be a perfect surprise and a touch of Indian tradition. I merely heard all the talk, engrossed in my own thoughts—so there was Arvind Singh, the man who had almost ruined my life.

4

THE ASMA GIRLS

t was another winter morning; three girls were having a gala time sitting on the stairs of the National Library, Alipore, Kolkata. They were singing some popular numbers of the Hindi movies like – *'aaj mein upar asma niche'*, *'awara bhamre jo hole hole gaye,'* *'dil hai chotasa chotisi asha.'* Yup, one of them was me, Lathika during my university days. We were the popular girls in the campus, the asma girls. The trio- Lathika, Tanya and Isha had bunked their classes that day to rehearse for their performance in the university cultural event that year. For some reason Tanya was singing quite off-track that day, she seemed lost in one of those infamous mood.

Isha, the tall, talkative, flamboyant girl burst out in anger, "What are you doing Tanya?"

Tanya, the quite soft spoken girl uttered something of which we had no clue. Tanya said Arvind, the ex-Xaverian and Kunal, the ex-Ashutosh guys were following her around the campus all day long for the last three days. She even heard them passing comments like- *ayey hai, kya chaal hai, hum to fida ho gaye*[18].

Isha shrugged her shoulder and was about to say something, when I interrupted. I knew both these girls long enough, they were polls apart. I had always mediated whenever there was discord between them; as such they often referred me as 'smarty.' I stood up from the stairs like a despotic ruler to dictate the group as if we were about to launch a war. Of course this was no less than a war because this was the matter of our prestige; after all we were the popular Asma Girls.

"Oh what a disgrace, we must protest. We must do something, we must teach them a lesson, a good one, and how dare they tease you Tanya," I was adamant.

"Take it easy smarty; it's not the time to lose temper rather to think rationally."

"What do you mean? We will do nothing?"

Isha appeased, "We will, but first let's watch them for sometime and then we will decide what to do."

Tanya agreed, "I think she is right."

Now who could argue against them, finally the two poles were coming together on something, so I smiled and nodded my head in affirmation, "But with one condition. I will get to slap them if we catch them red handed."

---

[18] Oh! What bearing you have, it has floored me

18

Then we chalked out a plan, how we would leave Tanya alone at library and let them follow her. Then we would follow those idiots and catch them then and there. But for the next four days there was no action from the enemy front. May be they were cautious, though we behaved normally. Then finally our big day came. It was the day of our performance at the cultural event of our university at the college street campus. In the early hour, when we were getting ready, Isha spoke, "Tanya we have been practicing too hard for this day. So you better be good. Don't mess up."

The last line had provoked Tanya, "Why are you saying this only to me, isn't she performing with us too."

Isha was always defensive of me, she said, "She never messes up, but you do."

Tanya, "Ok then, two of you perform, I am quitting."

"Easy babes, this is time for us to prove to the rest that we are the best." I tried to be funny by saying, "See even that rhymes so well."

They laughed together and that set our mood. The performance was too good and much appreciated; people joined in the songs and danced to it. We decided not to wait till the end of the program else we might get really late reaching home. It was at the bus-stop the Asma girls had to separate in different directions for our respective destinations. We wanted to chat a little more, so we skipped four buses intentionally. Then I heard someone from behind.

It was Arvind, "Hey girls you were pretty good at the show. Congrats!"

He walked ahead turned and extended his hand for a shake. Only Tanya, the dumbo, had to accept and shake the hands of the snake. He smiled, "And you were especially good as you added the *alaap*[19] to the song 'asma…' That was really innovative."

Tanya was overwhelmed, "Really, oh thank you."

They were still talking when I and Isha boarded our respective buses and left. Next day when I reached the Alipore Campus I couldn't find them anywhere. I went to the national library where I saw them fighting over something. As I approached them, Isha said, "Lathika tell this bitch she is no more one of us."

Tanya shouted back, "You jealous moron, you are jealous because he is interested in me not in you."

Matching decibels Isha answered, "Oh, what cheek! I have better guys in my life than that stupid idiot woman stalker."

That reminds me that Isha was actually dating one of our professors, the only eligible bachelor in our department. Every Saturday she would wear sari get decked up and enter Professor D.C. Dutta's chamber and spend the whole day discussing politics and more. I was lost in my thought when I heard Tanya saying, "Well say something, will you?"

I was perplexed, "What?"

Isha was demanding, "Well, choose a side. Who do you want to be with for the rest of the year?"

---

[19]   The preceding notes that set the mood of the main song

I shouted back at them, "You crazy girls! How could you divide so easily, that too for a guy who hardly matters to us? Hello! We are the asma girls, the popular girls. We must not fight over silly things but stick together because, because..."

I was wracking my brain for a valid reason when Tanya came up with one, "Because we love each other."

"Yes, that's true, I am sorry Tanya," apologized Isha.

Yes I made it again, achieved the impossible. I tell you it's very easy, especially when you confuse people with emotional words like 'love', 'friendship' etc. For the moment we thought nothing could come between us, till the idiot Arvind used the 'divide and rule' strategy on us. Tanya was being friendly with Arvind and we were missing her amongst us in the usual hangout place.

"So they are friends now," commented Isha.

"Best friends I believe," I agreed.

"We must do something."

As if I was waiting for her to say this. So I jumped up at-once, "Yes. I have a plan."

Isha looked confused, "What plan?"

I explained her plan and explained every minute details how to execute it.

Isha asked doubtfully, "You think this won't be too dangerous right? What if the professors come to know about it?"

"No it won't, unless you tell it personally to your favorite professor."

Then we laughed out loud in manly voice "Hah hah hah."

5

THE SWEET DISASTER

*F*inally arrived the stipulated day when we put our plan to action. It was one such usual Saturdays when most of our classmates stayed back home to study, as the Part 1 exam was just around the corner. Though the classroom gallery looked half occupied and half empty, we knew this was the best opportunity, especially when Tanya too skipped classes that day. We heard she was busy helping her family to arrange her elder sister's wedding. Her elder sister was also a C.U. student who was marrying her exclassmate. I told myself, "Now I know what Tanya was up to, probably to keep this tradition."

I felt agitated when professor D.C.Dutta entered the classroom with his usual disturbing noise from dragging his shoes 'khash, khash, khash'. I didn't miss Isha's smile on seeing him. Then he started his lecture on something that seemed so alien that I felt like evaporating. It was one such boring lectures on recent politics precisely dialectics of political leaders. It was becoming too hard to keep my sleepy eyes open when I heard Arvind interrupting with an insightful, intellectual question, "But Sir, you cannot generalize... blah blah blah." The class seemed mesmerized and clapped; I too had to join them. It felt like appreciating a modern art, you may not understand it but have to appreciate or else you will be considered dumb.

Finally the bell rang much to my relief. At once everyone got busy packing away their books or moving out; it was time when I had to execute my plan. Isha patted my shoulder and I walked slowly across the stairs from first bench to the fifth row where Arvind was sitting with his friends.

"Hi Arvind, may I have a word with you for a second?" I asked.

Arvind coolly shrugged his shoulder, "Yeah! Sure."

His other friends whisked off the place as if they knew what was coming. Suddenly I went on my knees and in a timid tone said, "I love you Arvind, I love you too much believe me."

He was under shock when I added, "Please don't be angry and please leave Tanya alone, hope you will understand."

I was about to pour out more but then he said, "Ok, ok."

And he ran off scared to the bone. All boys are like that, they prefer to run off if they fail to handle a situation. I said to myself, "Here goes our hero, the ex-Xaverian, who was almost unbeatable until now."

I came down to my seat in the first row and Isha secretly shook my hand - Mission Accomplished! For some reason I was shivering. After the bell rang classes resumed. I was a bit worried as Arvind and his friends were not there. What if they are planning a counter attack? I firmly held Isha's hand till I reached the bus stop. I took a cab immediately because I had to escape from the premises as quickly as possible. I was feeling very guilty but preferred to stay calm.

As I reached home I felt a little better with mom hugging me and kissing me like she does every day when I return. I was about to walk into my room when mom informed Isha had called at our land phone, "Hello Isha."

"Hey my *desi*[20] Julia Roberts, how are you doing?"

I knew Isha too was worried about me, so I said, "That was quite a Julia Roberts moment for sure! But for a change this time Richard Gere ran off in fear."

Isha seemed to enjoy at my remark, "Huh! He is not even close to Richard Gere."

We laughed together for a while. Then she promised to stay strong by my side, before she hung up.

Next morning I went to the university campus with the anticipation of being humiliated by all, after all it's a mass psyche to target the weak. So I held my head up and gallantly walked through the corridor when I heard Tanya calling from behind, "Lathika, I heard what you did to Arvind yesterday."

---

[20]   native

It sounded as if I had molested him. I kept mum though, as she continued, "You know how much he respected you, how much he liked you?"

"What? Don't tell me he loved me!"

"Yes, he always enquired about you whenever we met."

"I give a tiny rat's ass to it," I protested vehemently.

Then I saw tears rolling down her eyes, "You, you heartless bi…"

"Don't you dare pronounce the word."

I raised my finger to her. Tanya ran away to the library.

Damn! I stamped my foot on the ground and then moved ahead towards my classroom. I felt others gazing and whispering behind me. The girls must be thinking- so cool, she's got some guts. While the boys stared–'she is really hot man, so hot that Arvind almost evaporated.'

I was prepared for all of this; it's like living in the spotlight. I don't remember what happened for the next few days as I was too busy with my studies, even though I noticed Arvind was absent throughout that period. I started to feel bad and after much thought I went up to Kunal, the fat friend of Arvind, "Excuse me Kunal."

"Now what do you want?"

"Can you tell Arvind that I am sorry, I mean extremely sorry, it was just a stupid bet you know." I blatantly lied and I saw I was clearly making an impression as he smiled.

"Ok I will tell him," Kunal said.

I left with a 'thanks'.

Then the next day I saw him in the campus again, it reminded of an old Bengal phrase- *phool phutuk na futuk aaj basanta*[21]. He was having a crepe bandage in his left arms, a perfect excuse for his absence. But he looked very different, more confident than ever, as if he had undergone some kind of training to deal with harsh reality! Huh! But I was in no mood to fight with him as I had already lost two of my best friends in that foolish act of mine. The back stabber, Tanya had joined Arvind and his team in the fifth row, while Isha was too busy with the professor and hardly attended class. The one incident that was supposed to bind us together actually did the opposite. My plan backfired. We were drifted apart forever. I had lamented for a while, but then I realized it's just a waste of time.

Then we passed the exam with flying colors and as the new class started I made some new friends. Time had perhaps made deeper impact on me; I became very studious all of a sudden. I chose Contemporary India as my alternative paper over Research Methodology, knowing the back benchers would obviously select the later for their future study i.e., PhD. And I was right; they are so-o-o-o-o predictable! This year I paid least attention to others and concentrated on my grades, it was very important for me. And finally came the day when we bid goodbye to each-other. I remembered how Isha dragged me to the classroom that day. She said, "Now you two shake hands and make up."

Tanya and I had to follow her command. Then to make the day memorable we took a picture of us together, which stayed with me in my album, I called 'end of an era'.

---

[21]   Even if flower doesn't blossoms, still it's spring today

6

THE PACT

uddi gushed, "Mashi are you listening to me?"

I was instantly out of my reverie, "Yes I am, my dear."

"So are you in?"

I had no clue what was she talking about but I nodded, "Yes I am very much in."

Then we did a high five.

"This is so cool," said Guddi.

Her excitement was at the peak. I was about to probe into the reason behind it, which got suddenly interrupted as Dad shouted, "Out, out, out."

Before this we almost had forgotten his presence. Now with the dismissal, discussion shifted from wedding to the current India-Pakistan Test match that was being telecast. I was swiftly moving towards my room when I heard Ryan say, "What is so interesting about cricket isn't it the same old stuff?"

Guddi smirked, "You wouldn't understand it. We girls just love to watch good looking men in uniform running around in front of us."

"You are so appalling."

"So are you, I saw you watching porn the other day!"

"When?"

"Gotcha!"

"You bad girl."

"He he he."

"Ha ha ha."

I smiled from a distance and blessed them a lifetime of happiness together.

It was around 11.30 when we had our dinner. And then as soon as Ryan left, I went to my room, fell flat on the bed with a plan to wake up late the next day.

I was having a bad dream, a scary one precisely, where a giant was about to gulp me alive. Suddenly my voice was choked and I was struggling hard to open my mouth. My nightmare got abruptly aborted with a sound of banging on the door. I checked my watch, it was 7.30 a.m. still in the mood to sleep some more. I asked, "Who is it?"

"Open the door mashi." It was Guddi.

I hurriedly opened the door, "What is it Guddi?"

"You are not ready yet?"

I was still very dizzy, "Ready? Why?"

"Oh mashi you promised, you promised last night. They have already arrived and you are saying…"

She was about to cry, so I somehow managed, "Hey, hey, I was just joking, give me two minutes and I will be ready."

"Two minutes mashi only two minutes."

I nodded in affirmation. As I closed the door again to get dressed I said to myself- oh boy! She gets on my nerves sometimes.

I knew this is going to be a sunny day, so I dressed up in light colored clothes. A white shirt and light blue jeans and some accessories. I came out with a broad smile on my face, "Hey everybody I am ready."

Much to my surprise a middle-aged couple standing across the hall-way replied in unison, "Hey-y-y-y!"

I guess these were Ryan's parents.

The man approached, "Finally we get to meet you. I am Stanley and here is my wife Rosalini."

I replied with warmth, "Pleasure meeting you both."

Guddi came running with Ryan, "Wait, wait, wait let me introduce you to my only mashi, the good girl of our house."

In the next few minutes we were all settled in the family car, heading towards Birla Planetarium, from there to Victoria Memorial, then to Alipore Zoo and then we will go to New Market where we will have lunch and next obvious destination 'Fame' for a Hindi Movie.

Guddi was sitting at the front next to the driver. She turned back, "This was our pact that Mashi and I have been planning for a long while."

I wondered when I made such a silly pact with Guddi. But had to comply with her, "Oh yes, yes the pact."

As we reached Birla Planetarium I saw a phuchkawala standing at the corner. Ryan's Mom enquired, "What are those round balls?"

I said, "A tasty delicacy of Bengal, why don't you try some?"

"Why not!"

Stanley joined in, "Yes I will have it too."

They were gulping phuchkas one after another and simultaneously uttering 'delicious'.

The phuchkawala urged, "Ma'am, have some more. It's good for digestion."

I was surprised, "You know English?"

The phuchkawala smiles, "Yes madam, I am a graduate. But you see this is my family business."

I nodded with a smile. Then Ryan took some photographs of the phuchkawala and us. As we walked along the street to our next destination I saw Ryan trying to make a conversation with me. When everyone was walking ahead, Ryan stepped near me and said, "I am sorry mashi."

I knew this was coming because I had seen his pale face since the last night stepping on wrong foot mishap. To cut the awkwardness I patted his shoulder, "C'mon. I didn't mind. You are a nice boy Ryan."

7

HOROSCOPE MATCHING

It was nearly 9.30a.m when we reached Victoria Memorial. After a couple of photo sessions in front of the entrance gate we finally entered the premises. As we walked along the lanes, I scanned through the serene sight. "It looks all the same" – I murmured to myself. Rosalini faintly nodded. She looked at me with great interest probably expecting some delightful stories of this place.

Though I visited this place many time as a child with Mom and Dad mostly on New Year's Day, like an old ritual, I couldn't recall anything exciting to tell Rosalini that would interest her.

It was one such New Year about a decade back and the world was in a celebration mood. I woke up in the morning getting a tight hug from Mom and with that she would transfer all her positive vibes in me. "Mom when are we going to the Victoria Memorial, the Queen must be waiting for us." I thought this will bring some more smile to her face. But she seemed to be in her rare pensive mood. So I enquired, "Is everything alright Mom?"

She replied in a melancholy tone, "I am worried about your Dad." I knew what she meant, so I patted her shoulder consoling, "He will be fine mom, he will be fine."

Somehow those words gave her courage and she smiled, "Ok get up now, we will leave by 10.30 and here take this, you wear this salwar suit with my newly stitched matching hanky."

I was really delighted because she not only knew my taste but always had a matching handkerchief to go with every dress. That much she cared. No one had loved or cared about me as much as she did. That day we had followed the usual program of visiting places; parks and theatre halls. It was crowded everywhere. We were very happy too. At that moment Mom started singing out loudly, "*Ei akashe amar mukti aloye aloye*[22]". I joined keeping the beat. Then I saw dad who had already bypassed us and walking ahead at a distance seemed so embarrassed that he pretended as if he was not with us! We mocked him all our way back home from Victoria Memorial. But Mom and I both knew that Dad was really disturbed and nothing we did could please him. Actually he was worried for quite a while. It was almost four years he has been trying to find a good match for me but all his endeavors seemed to fail. By then I had already passed my masters

---

[22]   A popular Song by Rabindranath Tagore

and joined a leading national newspaper as a Copy Editor. I was enjoying my life. I had already made new friends and with them I was experiencing a new life. I tried new things like –smoking cigarette that too menthol flavored; I drank something called Teachers and went to the disco theque where I danced like a gorilla. Once, my friends showed their inclination to visit my parents as I already had told them how supportive they were of all my decisions. Alright it was partly true. And when they finally visited my house Dad roared like a tiger, "Here comes our Mokhhi Rani[23]!"

He said this because I was accompanied by my colleagues and most of them were men! He scared them away from the front gate. I too felt like running with them, but gathered enough courage and stepped on the door mat that had inscribed 'Home Sweet Home'. He was shouting his lungs out. Most of which meant how I brought shame to the honor of his family. My head felt like exploding and then Mom came up with a fantastic idea. Suddenly the mixer grinder roared. At first dad got confused but as he tried to start his second session, the motor roared on a higher note. Dad could hardly compete with that, so he left the scene in a huff! We now had a new weapon in our hand, whenever the poor man opened his mouth; the scary mixer grinder challenged him. But again there is an old saying- 'You must not fight too often with one enemy or you will teach him all your art of war.' So next time the mixer roared the TV was tuned to highest volume to

---

[23] Queen bee

counter the attack. We had waged war against each other, the World War III!

But whose fault was this, if you try to analyze the situation. Mom and I were on a defensive mode while it was Dad who started it all. No one could blame him for that because for the last four years he was trying desperately to marry me off; maybe he was being too hard on himself. Day in and day out he would scan newspapers, matrimonial websites, contact them, request them to visit us and after the round of fashion parade in front of them, they would leave saying 'Sorry Sir but we don't think she would be fit for our son.' He wondered what was wrong with his daughter. Then he came to a conclusion, "You are fat!"

This made Mom angry, "Don't you dare call her fat, she is average built."

So that was me, in my late twenty's, quite pretty and attractive, I know it for sure. Mom was so beautiful that, if she were into Movies she would have been just next to Suchitra Sen[24]. I was a carbon copy of my Mom, most relatives and friends confirm that. I was also quite homely, I knew how to cook, keep the house clean that could qualify me to be a good bride but nothing seemed to work. Then one day dad came up with another reason, "It's her stars that's creating hindrance to her prospective marriage."

Then an Astrologer came to our house as a great savior. I was peeling potatoes in the kitchen when I heard

---

[24]   Famous Bengali film star

him saying with a sigh, "Oh she is *Mangalik*[25]!" In my anger I peeled off the best portions of the potato as if I was tearing off that smelly skin of the astrologer. Then he called me up, "Come my girl, let me look at your palm."

I smashed the soap container as I walked out of kitchen intentionally to show my anger. But thank God the container did not fall else I would have to clean up the mess. The astrologer predicted that soon there will be good news for the family. Probably by that year in August I will be married in to a good family. But still there was a little problem, there might arise some problems in future for that I have to wear some stones, zodiac stones. As soon as he left I was about to make a drama. But then I saw dad's face he seemed very happy. Finally I saw a smile on his face. When I went back to my room Mom was busy cleaning up. Folding clothes neatly, putting away books in the shelves, night suit ready at the corner of the bed, while the bed sheet was perfectly stretched. When she finished, she looked up, "How does it look now?"

I replied in a repulsive tone, "It's all the same," and I bumped on the bed and crumpled the bed sheet, "I hate him, I hate him, I hate Daddddddddd!"

---

[25]   Born on a Tuesday under inauspicious stars

8

THE UNHAPPY ALLIANCE

*I*t was in mid-February when Dad finally had a breakthrough. He heaved a sigh of relief and spoke with utmost enthusiasm, while I listened with equal disinterest. They had called the Ghosh family; they said the horoscopes had matched.

I couldn't react to it, though Dad continued, "You know what that means? Finally our daughter will be married off to her prince charming."

He was probably expecting an overwhelming reaction from Mom, who looked quite lost at that moment. He then walked towards the bed where she was sitting and gave her a tight hug, "Shikha say something. Your Lathika will be finally going to her own house, are you not happy?"

Then he lifted her face with the right hand and leaned forward. I was sitting next to Mom, when I caught that sight of horror! I thought was he going to kiss mom, oh God! Spare me the horror. Reality Byte- its one thing to see people kissing in movies which you actually enjoy but watching your parents making out, even in your dreams is unbearable. I quickly retorted, "But Mohan Ghosh is hardly a prince. That donkey faced, uneducated smelly ass."

My harsh words diverted dad's attention, "Mind your language young lady! I know that he is the right match for you."

I almost jumped on the bed and stood in an arrogant posture, hands tightly under the arms and nose up in the air, "I don't think so!"

Dad went red in anger, "Who are you to decide what's right and wrong for you? I am here to do it for you."

"This is so unfair!"

Mom now broke her silence, "Enough of this, stop this at once and apologize to your father."

I was totally confused with her reaction. She never spoke to me like that ever before. My father's face had brightened up with the Mom's support. He smiled, "It's okay darling, she is just a child. She doesn't know what is good for her; we will be her guiding stars till she is old enough to understand how much we love her."

I had nothing more to say, my fate was sealed. So I left the scene in agony.

It was 6th August 2002; I was totally excited when I woke up. Not because I was getting married that day, Reva, Jiju- Bhaibhav Bhattarai and Guddi, my little ten years old niece had already arrived from Mumbai. My new life was about to begin and I was bidding a final goodbye to my family, my home, my belongings and most importantly Mom. Mom had been my constant source of inspiration and support all my life. It was too hard to imagine life without Mom around me. I knew it was going to be very tough.

I was all the more worried when Reva added to my tension with a strange advice, "Little sis, remember in life never compromise but make proper adjustments." I nodded.

Then the ceremony began. Everyone around me the relatives, friends, colleagues all seemed so happy. Even I was happy but something was still bothering me. Mom was not allowed to witness the wedding for some strange rituals. I gestured Reva to come near me and whispered into her ears, "I will bring revolution someday against this discrimination against women."

Obviously Reva knew why I was so disturbed, so she pacified, "Okay sis, first get married and then try out all your methods on your hubby."

She smirked. I looked at the man sitting next to me from the corner of my eyes. He looked extremely handsome at that moment. I thought perhaps Dad was right in this decision. I almost had cried, well almost, out of gratitude. Then it was time for *Kanakanjali*[26], which I performed with Mom. I was about to board the groom's car and as I turned back for the last time, something extra-ordinary happened. I saw 'Hitler' crying.

---

[26] The ceremony of the new bride leaving her parent' house to go to her in-law's house

Thereafter a series of rituals took place at my in-law's New Alipore residence; I was too tired but religiously performed them all. I was very happy, unaware if the disturbing reality awaiting me in the near future. It all started just after the relatives left the house, I mean my new home. We the newly wedded couple had finally got our private space. We were busy in some intimate conversation when my mother-in-law barged into the room without a courtesy knock, '*Bouma*[27]', doesn't your father knows that you are married now and you have your own life? Why does he keep calling every half an hour to know how you are doing?"

She went on and on, I nodded like a little girl getting punished for not completing her homework. May be she found it amusing so she continued with her repugnant comments whenever she got a chance in the next few days. However, soon the day of rejoining the office arrived much to my glee. It was my big escape from the furor at home. But every day when I came back from work the same stuff would continue. "See the memsahib has returned. I was wondering what took her so long. Maybe she was too busy to save the world from alien attack," would be her sarcastic comment.

I was beginning to appreciate the ingenuity of her thoughts, when father-in-law interrupted, "Shhhh… darling don't talk to her like that, or our son will be angry."

Mother-in-law, "I curse myself for bringing this woman to our family."

---

[27]   Son's wife is addressed as 'Bouma' by parents

I exclaimed, "What have I done?"

"You keep complaining to our son about us."

The scene would have taken a dramatic turn, but my husband arrived and my in-laws chose to behave and be at their best. He had called from outside the gate in his usual tone, "Ma-a-a-a, B-a-b-a open the door."

I rushed downstairs and opened the door with a broad smile. He totally ignored me and walked straight up to his parents', "Ma, baba, you know what happened today ..."

I was feeling really disturbed so I thought to confront him that night, "Darling why didn't you recognize me standing there at the doorstep?"

"Sure! I saw you standing like an '*ullu*[28]'," he smirked.

"Don't you care about me?"

"What do you mean? You are so jealous of my parents. Don't you realize they are old and they wait for me all day long till I return? You see I have some responsibilities."

"What about your responsibilities towards me?"

"Well, you have all my nights."

He gave a naughty smile but I was in no mood to continue the unpleasant conversation. Then he got busy surfing the TV and texting simultaneously. It was around 2.30 a.m he was still watching FTV when he enquired – "Are you asleep?"

"Why?"

"Come close, I want to have sex with you."

"Disgusting!"

---

[28]   Owl

I turned away. But the episode didn't end there, it continued like any mega – series on TV. Next morning I got some lessons in sex from my in-laws at the breakfast table. Obviously by then Mohan had left for office.

My mother–in–law asked, "Is there anything wrong with you? Don't think my son said anything to us, but we sense his dissatisfaction from his face."

My father–in–law advised, "Don't you be so frigid all the time. Your mother-in-law knows all the tricks to woo a man, try to learn some from her."

My over enthusiastic mother-in–law was about to reveal her tricks, "Why don't you wear designer lingerie that will surely excite him."

They had to cut short the interesting conversation because I had to leave for office. Though in my way, I sent a text to Mohan- 'I am sorry.'

Mohan texted back – 'for what?'

I wrote– 'your mother said that I failed to make you happy'.

Mohan didn't reply. And I was quite apprehensive what would happen next. Mohan didn't talk to me and slept on the floor that night. And the following night and the next night. I could not understand what to do, so I made a blunder by calling up Mom. She obviously narrated the incident to dad that made him call Mohan, during office hours to invite him for a family lunch at his place the coming weekend. That one phone was enough to start an inferno. So as I returned home, I was surprised to see all three sitting together and intensely discussing their next course of action.

I wanted to ease the tension, "Hey everybody!"

Mother-in-law sounded aghast, "Chi, chi, chi shameless woman. You discuss your private life with your parents?"

I didn't know how to react to it, should I laugh or cry. But that day I decided not to disclose any of my secrets to my parents. So yet another day passed with little hope of better tomorrow.

My routine life continued for three months. Mohan had never kissed me or hugged me to express his love. By then I realized that Mohan and I was never on the same page, rather he lagged far behind in everything that mattered to me. He had no interest in politics, sports, art and creativity, not even in love. His most sensible discussion always started with Ambedkar and how great a man he was.

His parents were even awe struck with their son's intellect. But undeniably he scored high in one subject i.e., sex. He seemed to be always in the mood. Every now and then pulling me inside the room and taking his pants off he would say – "Quick, quick take off your nighty."

But mamma darling is always a spoil sport – "Shona, come we have something to show you."

The obedient son would run out, of course, pulling back his pants, "Yes mamma I am coming."

It was one such Sunday morning; I woke up a little late. I heard a bang on my door, "Your parents are here, come and meet them."

I was surprised and then I recalled, I had a conversation with Reva the day before but I hardly told her anything about my life. It was just innocent "hmm". That was enough reason to take away peace from my parents' life. My mouth was wide open as I stood in front of them.

Dad came forward and hugged me tight, "How are you doing shona?"

I tried to fight my tears but failed, "Oh dad!"

When they finally settled down in a more or less comfortable position, my in–laws started accusing them.

"Both of you had lied to us; you did not tell us that your daughter is suffering from a severe illness," accused my mother–in–law.

My parents almost exclaimed in unison, "What illness?"

Father–in–law said, "You didn't tell us that she had constipation."

9

MARD-KA-BACHCHA

Fifteen days had passed since I had walked out of my in–laws' house with my parents.

I was back in my old room which seemed to welcome me with its old warmth. I was happy and feeling relieved like a free bird. But my guiding angels seemed so defeated all the time, especially my dad. Though he never told me anything but I could sense his helplessness. Sometimes I wanted to walk up to him and say, "It's ok dad, I am fine now, you saved me from the miseries. You are my hero, I love you." But somehow I could not gather the courage to speak up to him.

Gradually there was something changing inside me. I had mellowed down considerably. Slowly I was coming closer to God; no day would start without making a proper prayer to Him. I thanked him for everything though I knew there were more tests left for me in life. I was ready to face them.

So one day, when my Editor called me to his room I knew what was coming.

He grinned with his funny face and leaned on the table in front of him, "You see Lathika I really don't have a complaint against you. But you don't seem to be the same girl we admired, where are the sparks?" He paused to check my reaction.

I listened calmly as he continued, "You have a bright future. I can help you with that but you have to be a bit more cooperative, you see."

Again he glanced at me, so I had to nod. He felt more confident now, "You don't open up to me like others. You should always come to my cabin and we can discuss like others."

I couldn't take the crap any longer, "Like others?"

And then I walked out of his office submitting my resignation. The impromptu of my action, was a direct slap on the Editor's face. As I walked out of the office building, I said to myself that day, nothing more can go wrong, not because there is nothing left but I had learnt to trust myself. I promised that I would never give up on myself.

So now I was unemployed, separated and happy. I had no idea what to do with my life. I was, for the first time, living at the moment and for the moment. "Ah this is life, so beautiful why didn't I notice before?"

I was beginning to get carried away with my new found freedom when I bumped into Arvind, one day, at a Mall in South Kolkata. Soon we ended up catching up over coffee.

He almost burst out, "*Agar who mard ka bacha hota*[29], he would have never let you go like that. He would have stood by your side in high and low."

Well, that was enough reason for me to trust him again. So we started meeting every other day which was followed by long conversations on the phone. My parents knew something was going on, but they never intervened. Maybe they were happy because I was happy. In another meeting with Arvind I told him that I was thinking of returning to my in-laws' place because they too were calling to solve the matter.

Arvind blew up, "Are you crazy? You don't deserve this. You need a real man to take care of you."

"And who is that man? You?"

I casually said that and he said, "Yes, I will take care of you for rest of your life. Marry me."

"You know I am still not legally free yet."

"So get a divorce."

I jumped off my seat, "What?"

Arvind smiled, "Yes, I love you Lathika."

I tell you, life is so full of surprises. Someone up there is writing new stories and adding new chapters in our life. I believe the creator loves his creation so much; he too wants to meet them in person. May be I will get the privilege of meeting him some day. Or maybe I had encountered Him when He gave a second chance to me.

All this might sound little vague and abstract, until I continue with what happened next. So Arvind and I

---

[29]   Had he been a man

both started happily planning our life together. We were roaming around New Market area bargaining and buying utensils for our new home. All along, Arvind kept on insisting, "It's about time you should talk to your parents."

"I will, I will."

When I went back home I was still unsure if I wanted to talk to them. At dinner I spoke up with a quivering voice, "Mom, Dad, I think I want a divorce."

Dad consented, "If this is what you want, we will support you in your decision. We want to see you happy again."

I expected Mom to join, but she simply gave a blank expression. Later that night she finally spoke, "What's going on shona?"

I could have lied or denied but I confessed, "Mom I met Arvind at the Mall and......."

She didn't tell me anything after I had completed my part of the story. But looking at her eyes I knew she didn't like the Arvind character emerging back in to my life. But it was pretty late; I had fallen asleep in her lap and the whole night she remained awake. Her hand was moving softly across my hair and she was chanting hymns.

Like I already said, I was doing exactly what Arvind wanted me to do. I was completely under his spell. The day I filed the case for my divorce, he thought it would be great if we celebrated it with a booze party. Initially I had rejected it like another bad idea but he knew how to convince me with his sweet talks. We went to a hotel cum restaurant; let's call it hotel Decent, together we enjoyed decent glasses of beer. Arvind smiled and said, "Come with me, I have booked a room for us." I knew what he meant, I pleaded, "No please no, not before marriage."

He whispered putting his finger on my lips, "Shh don't be scared, you know I love you and I will marry you as soon as you get the divorce. Don't you trust me?"

In the next few minutes I was in a hotel room and in his arms. It felt so right that I didn't think twice. It was quite an action packed afternoon. He was striking the unexplored chords with much caution and I was reciprocating to it with equal passion. I was still caught in the euphoria when I turned towards him and said, "I love you Arvind."

Arvind, who was panting heavily next to me, opened his eyes and gazed at the ceiling for a while.

"Hey Arvind, I told you, I love you."

Suddenly he started laughing out loud, "We are even now."

"What? What are you talking about?"

"Well, well, you ruined the best years of my life remember? So I screwed yours now, get it, Asma girl?"

I couldn't recover from the shock and I sat dumb struck watching him go away without even looking back for once. Next, I sneaked out of the Hotel, took a cab, reached home and locked myself up in my room.

I was completely shattered, my dreams, my future plans were mocking me. And like any stupid loser I did the obvious, I made an attempt to kill myself by cutting my hand with a razor blade and blacked out.

Then I heard someone saying, "Silly, Silly girl."

I smiled to hear him, so I struggled hard to open my eyes. I saw a young man wearing a white gown standing next to me –"Silly girl, you scared your parents." I gave him a confused look. He said, "Don't look so surprised, you are still alive and I am your doctor".

I looked around the room, felt happy to see some familiar faces among the nurses and attendants. "Mom, Dad I am so sorry."

"Good. Good realization. Wait, I have a surprise visitor for you, come my son."

Mohan entered and holding my hands said, "I never believed you could do such thing for me. I am so sorry Lathi, I promise I will never leave you alone again in my life. I love you so much." So he cried and then I cried. Dad cried and Mom cried. Even the doctor cried a little.

As promised, Mohan never left me for a moment since then. We had shifted our base to Bengaluru, because he thought it would be best for both of us to start afresh. For the last fourteen years Mohan and I are leading a happy life together. Definitely we had made some suitable adjustments, if not compromises, at the end of the day we had each other, that's all life is about, sharing each moment with someone you love. I mean someone who loves you or whatever.

10

PICTURE ABHI BAKI HAI

"Mashi," Guddi called out to me.

I scoffed at her, "What is it now?"

"You are stealing all the attention; you look so beautiful in this blue *jardosi*[30], that everyone is looking at you only."

I know blue works for me, but I smiled at her, "Don't be silly, it's your day and believe me I have never seen any bride as beautiful and gorgeous as you."

She didn't protest. I had planted a kiss on her forehead. As I turned towards Ryan, who was standing next to Guddi, I saw him making a puppy face. Weird Boy, now I have to repeat the entire thing with him too. I smiled at him, "You look absolutely perfect." He bowed down a bit

---

[30]   Heavily embroidered with golden thread

and I had to kiss his forehead, "Son, take care of Guddi and always remember…"

Well, I got interrupted with a sudden commotion at the entrance. Someone special had arrived. I knew he would be coming; I had sweet-talked Guddi into inviting her 'Hero' to this auspicious occasion. He took firm steps as he walked across the crowd, "Hello Supriya and Ryan, congratulations to both of you, wish you a happy married life."

Both Ryan and Guddi thanked him for coming. I was waiting impatiently for my turn. But after the formal greetings the discussion flowed to another rather interesting topic i.e. Arvind's next step to mobilize the youth and pressurize the system to take action in favor of the Bankstreet rape victim. I understood this would take sometime, so I patted him from behind, "Hey Arvind."

He looked around totally surprised, "Oh is that you Lathika?"

He instantly recognized me though. He looked unusually calm, while my anger smoldered. I guess fourteen years is not enough to heal your wound, but somehow I managed to hide my expression with a fake smile, "How are you doing?"

Well, at the back of my mind I knew how ridiculous it sounded, especially after I made my research on him last night. I knew almost everything about him. But unfortunately Google says nothing about his personal life, just that he is still single. Arvind didn't respond to my query rather scanned me from top to toe, "Lathi, you look stunning and ravishing."

"And you look all the same."

Well I surely meant that he looked old. Forty plus something, an average built, tall guy, wearing pajama and *punjabi*[31] with shawl, couldn't be described as handsome.

A momentary silence had prevailed when Guddi came as a rescuer, "Mashi, you never mentioned that you knew Arvind Sir, you bad girl Mashi."

We all started laughing as if she had cracked a joke. I was more elated at my smooth transformation from "Good Girl' to 'Bad Girl'.

Then Arvind spoke, "What are you doing now?"

Guddi replied to this, "Mashi writes poems, stories, dramas and and…"

She was searching for the exact word, when I said, "I'm writing a book."

"Ahh, a book…?" He paused for a moment then asked, "What is it about?"

I grinned, "Well, it's an autobiography."

His faced ashened instantly, when I shrugged, "Ok, enjoy the party, see you, bye."

I felt like a winner as I turned away and walked towards the exit. Arvind, who is always prompt with his plan called out, "Hey, Lathika."

I had to stop because I didn't want to make a scene at my lovely niece's wedding.

"Can we meet sometime… we can catch up with our good old times?"

---

[31]   A loose fitting long shirt up to the knees

"Yeah sure, why not, call me then." I paused and then added, "I still have the same number."

He seemed to be pleased. Then he added, "Say hello to your Dad for me. Tell him that I kept my promise."

I was surprised to hear his last words. "What promise?" I asked myself. I hurriedly walked towards the exit, where I saw Reva chatting with a fat guest."Where is Dad, Reva?"

Reva shrugged, "He's not here. You know where to find him."

When she said that, she looked and sounded so much like mom. I stood there for a moment when I felt a tear welling up; I took out my hanky from the vanity bag to smudge it. I was surprised to notice that the color of the hanky exactly matched my saree and then I burst into tears, "Mom I miss you!"

When I reached home, dad was in his room holding something in his hand. I knocked.

"Come in Lathika," he said.

I sat next to him, "Are you alright Dad?"

I wanted to say to him, 'It's ok Dad, you can cry, men can cry, and I too miss Mom.'

He nodded his head, which meant he is fine. He then took my hand and gave me an envelope, "It's for you; your mother had left this for you."

After a long pause, he heaved a sigh, "I hope you will forgive me after reading this."

I couldn't control my tears, neither could he. I said something with my chocked voice, "Dad I don't hate you. I love you."

He obviously didn't understand a single word, but he kept on staring at Mom's photograph, hanging on the wall of his room.

Ah! This is 24th January 2013; I am on my way back to Bengaluru. I was all alone in the cab, witnessing the beauty of the city in this winter morning. I was really happy as I was taking away a part of my Kolkata with me, my Mom's letter, though I hadn't read it yet. I felt like singing after so many years when I actually did- *Aaj mein upar, asma niche…*

As I got off the cab in front of the entrance gate of the national airlines, the driver said, "Didi[32], you sing really well."

"Thank you, thank you," I smiled.

I glanced at my wrist watch and realized I had enough time, so let me call Mohan. I knew he must be really angry as I didn't keep my promise to call him every night. But I was sure he would be doubly excited once he hears my voice. Suddenly, my mobile rang; it was flashing an unknown number. Obviously I knew this number so well, in spite of deleting it long back. So, Arvind did call; I was in a confused state of mind, I looked at it for some time in disgust- some people don't give up, do they? At the next moment I thought, "What if there is something important that he wanted to tell me." I was in my dilemma- 'should I take it, should I not.'

---

[32] Indians address elder sister as 'didi'

11

HEAVENLY ABODE

"*H*urray! Finally I am home."

Yes that was her first reaction when she landed at the Bangalore International Airport. Now that her phone was still not switched on she had no clue if Mohan had made it in time. Haunted by the thoughts of Arvind, though the time she spent was brief, she stepped outside the crowded exit. And here was Mohan standing with an unexpected guest. Ah! What a pleasant surprise - Misti had arrived for the holidays!

Both shouted out loud, "Mom, I missed you."

They walked towards the parking area. As nothing could match the most comfortable family *i10* car they eased themselves into it. I was still arrested in my thoughts which I wanted to hide from the others by abruptly staring here and there in the car. Mohan and Misti were smiling as if they had caught her red handed. Then Mohan explained, "It has been cleansed well, watch it carefully darling, no stains just as you love it." I was trying to craft a meaningful remark but only could say- hmmm, which of course went off quite well, at this Mohan and Misti high fived.

All through the journey Mohan spoke vehemently mostly about how he survived without me. Misti who was sitting next to her father in the front turned back to gaze at me, "You look stunning Ma." My long hair was making waves in the breeze and for some reason I was blushing. Mohan noticed through the rear view mirror, "What is it honey?"

I shook my head. Soon we reached our Koramangala Residence, which resembles a well-to-do household. Everything looked all the same except for one thing. There was a transition in the heart of the lady of the house. So many things jumbled up in my mind, I needed time apart from the windbag Mohan. The loving husband was obviously overwhelmed to have me back. He wanted to know every single detail that he had missed. I finally broke my silence, "It was a wonderful wedding but I am too tired now. I will tell you at the dining table." The obedient husband immediately approved.

Like most married women I found my much needed solitude in the bathroom. I spent uninterrupted three hours thinking what could be the promise, and why did Arvind call after all these years. Several thoughts kept pouring out and for a moment felt like crying when I heard laughter outside the bathroom.

I hurriedly stepped outside to see Misti talking to someone over the phone, "Guddi didi don't worry, Mom returned safe and sound. So tell me didi how come an atheist like you, performed all the rituals so religiously? What? You saw *Maa Kali*[33] by rubbing your forehead for 100 times while chanting her name, and you want me to give it a try. Hahaha you naughty didi. She then laughed and sang- didi *tera huya, abh mera kabh hoga?*[34]"

I slowly walked towards Mohan, busy with his laptop on the sofa, "Don't you think Misti has grown up a lot quite fast? She seems much more mature than me at her age."

"She looks just like you, the same eyes and same smile. I wonder why she doesn't have anything that resembles me." I feel hesitant every time Mohan brings up this discussion, "Oh! She has your temper. And she loves you most my dear, she is a perfect daddy girl."

"No, she loves you more, you are her true hero not me."

"No Mohan."

"You bet, then let's call her and finish this once and for all."

"Oh! Stop it."

I throw a sofa pillow at Mohan. Mohan grabs it and throws it back. Then started the pillow fight which found new intensity as Misti joined the fight.

"Whose side are you in?" asked Mohan.

"I am neutral."

---

[33]   Hindu Goddess
[34]   You are done, now when will my turn come?

"You talk like a politician." Then turning towards me, "What happened darling, come let's dine together like good old days."

It was a happy hour for the family; the family time is the best time in every household. Likewise we spent the entire time talking more and eating less though there was a surprise at the end. The homemade ice cream called the sinful desert. Its Mohan's secret to get me almost turned on. For Mohan it's not just a pleasant feeling to make me happy but he really wanted something else, "Let's make another baby dear, it's time for one more please." I am the clever one; I take oral contraceptives each time and avoid the awkwardness and complexities that might arise.

That night it was as if nothing was enough. Thrice we had intercourse and each time we craved for more. Mohan is always very sensitive in this matter, and confirms whether the feeling is mutual. I responded in the positive and pulled him closer for yet another round of peace. It was at dawn when we were half asleep and still locked up in each other's arms and legs; that there was a sudden knock at the door, "Wake up Dad, Mom ....both of you are missing the fun." I hurried into the bathroom, freshened up a bit, wore my house coat and opened the door, "What is it sweetie?"

Misti was ecstatic, "There is a *bandarwala*[35] outside; he is showing off his monkeys dancing and mocking everyone at the roadside. Come on."

---

[35] Man showing up his monkeys doing pranks for money

"Okay I will join you, but I have one condition. And am sure you know what is it?"

"Not again, Mom. I won't be joining you guys to the Bose's."

"Yes dear, you will and it's not an order but a request, please."

"Oh sweet blackmailer, now hurry."

We both almost ran out in order to watch the monkeys, which was rather fun. It's was one such mother-daughter moment which we rarely share as most of the time Misti stays at her boarding school in Darjeeling. I turned my eyes to have a look at her smiling face, which looked as innocent as a baby. She had this shine in her eyes which I assume she inherited from her father.

12

THE WELCOMING NEIGHBORHOOD

The Bose's were our family friends who had invited us at a homely party for celebrating my homecoming. They stay at the Purba Park, which is about 40mins from our residence. All along Misti pleaded to skip the invitation, "I hate them Dad, please Mom, they are nothing but big show offs. Their son Aryan is a big bore. Of all he is a science geek. Uhh."

We both could sense her uneasiness but we were hardly left with any option. I preferred to shut her off, "This is enough, not a single word I want to hear disrespecting our friends. Look you...."

"Come'on Lathi it's perfectly okay, let her express herself."

"This way you are encouraging this. You know for this only she has become a spoilt brat."

"And the way you are handling the situation isn't right either dear."

"I know what is right for my daughter unlike you, you irresponsible…"

"What is that supposed to mean?"

"Nothing, just nothing."

We were almost there so the conversation had to end. Now that we entered their house holding the image of a happy family, we had no clue what more was coming. Mr. and Mrs. Bose greeted us with their usual warmth. They introduced us to the other guests, some neighbors and some were office colleagues. And here comes the embarrassment which I had not anticipated before.

Mrs. Anjali Bose declared, "Hello everyone here is introducing to all, our own the famous writer Mrs. Lathika."

"Thanks Mrs. Bose, for such gigantic introduction but my book is yet to release. And you are already making the stir."

"You will have to present us with one copy as soon as you grab one."

"You will get the first copy Raghav-da."

Mr. Bose smiled, "Oh it will be our great privilege to be the first and beat the rest in the runner's bench."

We all laughed in unison at this delightful comment. No one noticed Misti, who was in no mood to mingle with them. She rather stayed back at home and had secretly

planned out her next course of action at her school. She
was in a reverie when she heard me enquiring about Aryan.
Aryan Bose the one name that annoyed Misti. According
to her he was an attention seeker. A donkey faced dull boy
who badly needs a cosmetic surgery of his big flat nose.
On the contrary she misses her friend Ravi, the charmer,
during this short tour home.

"Oh here comes our young scientist."

Yup, Misti thinks that is what they call him as he has
made a stupid helicopter for his science project in school.
He is what he is. Misti hardly cares but she had to because
their parents let them blend. This is the only boy whom
they allow to jell up because this is supposed to be a bong
connection. The boy slowly made his way through the
curious crowd across the room and reached near Miss
Pretty, "Hello," he said.

"Hi."

"So are you comfortable, are you enjoying the party?"

Misti just smiled, to which he added, "I know this is
getting a little beyond tolerance. Especially, as our parents
guide us as what to do and what not. Are we a bunch of
morons or what?"

Suddenly the coy boy was talking sense. Misti of
nowhere laughed out loud. Aryan could easily guess that's
the shortest route to her heart by cursing the parents. He
then went on, "You know how hard it is to be the first boy,
and it's like carrying a crown of thorns over your head
knowing people are watching or judging you all the time."

Everything was going quite the well. When of nowhere
Mr. Bose triggered the bullet, "Hello everybody, may I have

your attention please, I have an announcement to make."
At once Misti's heart sank in fear. Yes it's her greatest
nightmare which is coming to reality. Mr. Raghav Bose
continued, "I father of Aryan Bose, after taking formal
approval of Mr. and Mrs. Mohan beg to unite Misti and
My Son, two bright individuals in holy wedlock in the
future once they become adults. And as…"

His mind absorbing speech was aborted by Mom's
sudden intervention,"… subject to their consent."

"Oh come on dear they are just love birds can't you
see that. I can't tell about your daughter, but for Aryan he
speaks of Misti 24x7."

Aryan objected, "Uhh Dad."

Raghav smiled, "Okay hahaha."

Everyone started to clap and suddenly Misti was the
center of attraction. She looked around as though feeling
totally violated. She spoke quietly to herself- oh this is the
reason I was brought here.

Such was her reaction when a dented and painted eye
narrowed, it was Aunt Chatterjee who came as a rescuer,
"This is a complete imposition Raghav and they are so
young. This is their time to grow by learning and playing
not to put pressure on their minds with this relationship
factor. Let them enjoy their life."

Raghav felt disappointed, "Maybe you are right but it's
just a proposal. No one will pressurize them if they plan to
go other ways. Am I right Mohan?"

"Yes absolutely."

Then followed the ritual of dinning where the
whispering continued among the strange guests, who

had merely an idea what's going on. But they enjoyed the repugnant proposal made by Raghav. Some said it's their business ventures behind the alliance. Some said it's just a bong thing, to book a Bengali bride in advance. While some said the kids are in love.

13

REACHING THE AGE

I thought why Misti can't be like any girl of her age – who is interested in the opposite sex. So on their way home she tried to explain to her, "Negative attitude is like a punctured tyre you cannot reach anywhere, until you change it." The speech sounded like monologue with no remark or protest from any corners. So I preferred to keep mum. That night I made up my mind to coax Misti to such an extent that she finally agrees to our wish. Inside me I am always scared that my daughter might turn into a revolutionary someday. May be my thoughts are not mere fears of a worried mother. Surely Misti is made for something else. So with the motive to cajole, I entered the dark chamber i.e. my daughter's room. I found her sitting by the window while the calm wind softly touched her red cheeks which were burning with anger.

Misti said, "If you are here to console me, then it's gonna be total waste of time."

I sounded like a priest, "No my child. I am here to let to see the prospect."

"Mom you are the one who promised me to fulfill my dreams according to my wishes. And now you are becoming intolerable with your mental cruelty upon me. How can you forget your promise which you made when I was a kid?"

I had no words. Misti remembered everything much to my surprise. And I being a mother forgot the basic rules of motherhood. I kept quiet.

Misti understood that her mother is back to her senses. She declared rationally, "I am going back tomorrow Mom. I want to attend the glorious 26th January day with my friends and teachers at the boarding."

"As you wish."

I left the room in dismay. All night I hoped for a natural calamity or health disorder to occur as a reason to stop Misti for one more day. I just cannot let her go halfhearted like this. I knew something will definitely come up, or if everything fails the drama queen will try much tested method. I will put an onion under her arms all night which will bring fever by the next morning, guaranteed. Aha! Here I diverted my direction to the kitchen instead of her bedroom. Then Misti cried out loud- 'Maaaaa'. What now, I had no clue. I rushed to the dark chamber yet another time.

"Mom, see what mess I have made. What is this Maa, I don't know how but I am bleeding."

There were blood stains all over her bed.

I was ready for this day, "It's time sweetheart to see things in different light. Don't you remember how I taught you about this? There is nothing to be scared off baby. C'mon let me wash you first and then let's do the cleaning and I will sing you sweet notes to help you get some sleep. Okay."

"Okay Maa."

I understood that Misti might be tormented at this very moment. While ushering my motherly affection, something inside me rejoiced at the thought of mission accomplished. I looked at my daughter who was now asleep, calm and quiet, holding my hand tight in between the palms. I realized Misti my beautiful daughter is still a little girl. Holding back at her I promised quietly into her ears, "I will be always there for you."

There are moments in our lives when we realize how important it is to stand up to someone especially when that someone looks up to you with hope and admiration. Such was the case with me as I knew I will never measure up to the care and love ushered to Reva and me by my mother. But that night she definitely knew what is best for her daughter. I will let her follow her dreams and she will guide her through it. That's a mother's promise given the 50/50 chances she will keep it.

Misti stayed back for the entire week for it was really hard on her part to accept the new found reality. She had had the privilege of pampered parents who didn't even push her to return to the school. Rather they rejoiced at her decision. She felt weak most of the time and smelled pungent which irritated her the most. But there was another reason for her irritation. The plan of action at the school was put to halt due to her sudden sickness. Though, her friends called, with whom she chatted for hours but on 26th of Jan someone special called. It was Ravi, her dearest friend. She was excited to the limit. And their discussion was like this-

Him to her-Hey beautiful.

Her to him-Huh! Are you alright?

Him to her- Aha! I thought it was your mother.

Her to him- You jerk!

Him to her- Ha ha! Jokes apart how have you been? There is no fun without you. Our signature campaign had just started and…

Her to him- oh you already started it. I will come along soon maybe by tomorrow.

Him to her- Today could have been the action day but we missed it.

Her to him- Everything will work out fine, don't worry.

Him to her- Okay I believe in you. I will wait for your return, till then goodbye dear.

Her to him- Goodbye handsome.

Him to her- Aha!

After that call suddenly she gathered all her courage back and went ahead to pack up. We, her parents were just standing outside the room trying to figure out what just happened. Mohan enquired of me, "Do you smell something?"

"Yeah a Tom cat that might just called our princess and provoked her."

Mohan was surprised at my remark, "This is not even a satire."

"Yeah I know."

"You used to be so much fun. Now you have grown out of it."

"Trust me funny man I will make it up to you, first let me deal with this."

I slammed the door of Misti's bedroom and spoke with an agitating tone, "What's going on? Put an end to it immediately or I will handle it my way."

"What Mom? Suddenly you are behaving like a... a..."

I raised my hand in the air, "Stop! I am asking who is that boy and why were you addressing him as handsome?"

Misti pleaded, "Oh! Please Mom; don't tell me you were eaves dropping the entire conversation."

"I heard a little. I missed the part when you said 'I love you' to the boy."

"I never said that to him. On the contrary I protest your action. Say sorry immediately."

"What? But why? Okay, sorry I overreacted. Come give me a hug. I was just getting upset as you are leaving. I miss you so much."

"Oh Mom, sweet Mom, don't be upset."

Then Misti hugged me tight and Mohan joined us and hugged the two precious ladies in his life.

14

THE LETTER

*N*ext day, after Misti left for her hostel, started with regular activities.

In the morning when I went to the small puja room, adjacent to the main bedroom, ignited the incense stick and sang a holy song - *'om jai jagdish hare'*; I heard a commotion outside the room. I shouted out loud, "What's the matter Mohan?"

"Can I come in; I have something to tell you?"

"Not now, don't you see I am busy?"

"Don't worry even your God will be happy to see it. And promise I will enter with bare foot."

"You haven't taken a bath yet, you can't come."

"Then you come outside; I have a surprise for you."

"Surpriseeeeeeeee!!!! Wait, I am coming."

I somehow completed the puja rituals as fast as I could and folded my hands in the air praying for my family. I hurried out and stood impatiently in front of Mohan.

Mohan opened his briefcase and slowly laid his hand on a jewelry box, saying, "I have learned from somewhere that once in a while you should give your family a chance to feel remarkable. Here it is to my beautiful wife a chance to feel special."

I was almost about to faint, "It's a diamond necklace!"

"Yes it is, and you are worthy of it."

I was almost feeling weak on my knees and tears started to roll down my cheeks with gratitude. It was a speechless moment for me. While Mohan was babbling, "I know these tears are my gift, you don't know how much I am happy just to find you so elated with my token of love. Actually I wanted a moment alone with you, so I did not show it to you while Misti was here. This is my moment, the best moment which I am not ready to share even with our beloved daughter. She is always special to me; I can fulfill all her listed demands but what about my listless wife who counts on me, not on any asset. You know you had left me for only few days, those days I worked and worked and finally I got my promotion letter. That day I realized how much you understand my priority. Then why not I do something to make you happy even more?"

"Stop it you duffer. Now you are telling me you had a promotion. And you call me a drama queen. Come close, will you?"

Then we had a long goodbye kiss.

He had gone to the IT firm named Mphasis for work and this gives me the whole day to myself. Since I had taken off from my official work-from-home job of content writing now, I can do my unpacking and cleaning that was long due. Generally during this hour I prepare my articles alongside taking breakfast. I had quit regular official job since I had a bad experience back home with my editor. So I prefer this job, which was no less hectic yet rewarding.

Usually I am a workaholic but today, I was in a different mood. I was waiting to sink my teeth into the words written in the last letter from Mom. So as he left, I swiftly went back to my room and don't know why but locked myself inside. I wanted uninterrupted attention to every minute detail.

My Dear Lathika,

You are my lovely daughter whom I loved even more than my first child Reva. I don't hesitate to confess this hoping you will understand the heart of a mother since you are yourself a mother now.

Your father and I never stopped you from doing anything you wanted. We both loved you the most, though you might have some complaints against you poor old dad. You always looked at me with high. But it was me who took a step without your knowledge for your own good.

It was one time when you had tried committing suicide for that Arvind; he had come to see you at the hospital. He begged and begged for my permission to meet you at least for once. I and your father had forced him to stay away from you and made him promise to keep this a secret.

Arvind had left and never turned his face on you ever since. But when I was ill, I met him once at the hospital serving some poor women health campaign there. He said, "I am sorry to hurt your daughter, but I am sorry also because you never let me make the suitable correction." I confessed to him that I had no choice. He smiled and touched my feet and left.

My darling daughter that moment I thought I had made a blunder. But again, after few months I heard the news, the birth of your girl child. The news was delivered to me by Mohan who told me how happy you are these days. Then I knew I didn't make that much wrong.

May God punish me for not letting two loving spirit to unite. But please don't misunderstand your old helpless father and also have some mercy on my soul, even though I let you down.

Be happy always.
Only Yours,
Mom.

Suddenly I was feeling clueless. I had no idea how to react to this. So I sat idle for a while staring at the window, searching for an answer in my mind- why Mom why?

At once I decided to find out what really happened that night at the hospital. So I instantly picked up the telephone and dialed my home number. The maid Renu had picked up, "Oh didi you? But Mashi is out for the *bazaar*[36], should I ask her to call you back?"

---

[36]   market

If it was some other time I, Lathika would have rejoiced thinking the way the maid address her as 'didi and Reva as 'mashi'. But now is no time for this. I immediately enquired about Dad.

Renu, "Dada thakur is sleeping." Out of curiosity she asked further, "Is it urgent, should I wake him up?"

"Oh no. It's okay I will call later."

I was about to cut the line when she enquired how I was doing. In response I also had to ask how she and her two daughters doing these days. But what Renu said left me with huge concern without knowing what to do. Renu told that her daughter is married off to a village boy who had a tea plantation business. She said, "They are very greedy people didi. They are pressurizing for more dowries, and I am worried she is not safe out there."

At first I rebuked, "Why did you marry her against her wish to a village boy when she has grown up in Kolkata?"

Then I realized it's no point raising this issue, so I said, "Why don't you bring her back."

What Renu replied was far more complex than what I expected. "It's not easy to bring back my daughter as her in-laws refuse to let her go saying this will hamper their family prestige in the society. But they continue to torture didi, she cries whenever we call. What should we do didi, whom should we take refuge to? Please help us didi, pleaseeee."

"Okay okay, I will do something, don't worry."

After I disconnected the telephone I realized that she was left with no option but to call Arvind. After all it's a matter of one call and that too for necessity. I still was feeling hesitant as I was scratching with my nail the motif of the linen saree she was wearing. She was almost growing pink thinking- what if he still has the same feelings for her, even after all this years? Or else what could be the reason that he is still very much single?

Then I decided I would hide my real feelings which were nothing but a feeling of sympathy and nothing more than that. As what had happened in his life, rather in both their lives was destined by God. For fifteen more minutes I stood there idle in my thoughts. Finally I could gather the courage to pick up the phone and dial his number. It rang once and her heart pounced, I immediately disconnected the call. Just within seconds Arvind called back, "I knew you would call, how are you Lathika?"

"How did you know it was me?"

"A call from Bengaluru, that too at this hour in the morning, who else could have called. I know you must have been as excited as me after our first meeting at your niece's wedding. It's been years Lathika but I still feel the same about you, I …."

Lathika was deeply touched, so mildly replied, "I know what you mean, but I didn't call to discuss this. I need a favor."

"What is it my Asma Girl?"

"Please don't call me that, it's very irritating. Actually I called to tell you about Renu, the maid at my Kolkata house and her daughter who are in big trouble. You are the only one who can rescue them from their current situation. Or the situation might go out of control; the in-laws of Paro might torture her to death. Please do something."

"Don't panic Lathi. You came to the right person. I will look into it right away. But one thing I don't understand is how could you trust me so much after what we had?"

"I know everything. Mom left me a letter revealing all the realities."

"I understand."

"Everyone goes through tough times in their lives, Arvind. It's how you deal with it. Our relation also went under the scanner and we crossed the test of time with dignity and patience. Let's be friends once again."

"Friends?"

"Just friends."

"Just friends it is then. Ha ha-ha."

The discussion then continued for a while from topics ranging from moral and political ones. But I couldn't ask one thing that has been bothering me for some time. The big question is- why is Arvind not married? Is he still waiting for me, Lathika?

15

DIRECT ACTION DAY

Some people are born to rule, they have the gift to make difference in the whole society at large. Misti has such extraordinary talent. When she speaks everyone listens, when she commands everyone bows, when she walks everyone follows. She is a girl meant for bigger challenges much like her father. Now also he is still planning something big.

Actually Misti and her friends Ravi, Shahid and Manjula were planning a protest against the biology teacher. Not just a mass protest, to expel him from the boarding school. But also put up a lesson to all those who think they can go easy with any student.

The teacher, Mr. Rajiv Desai was very abusive in nature. She had been constantly disturbing girls in different ways, sometimes he smack them in the back, sometimes he rub their shoulder and even touch them inappropriately. It went to the highest peak of intolerance after an incident that affected Manjula.

It was one sunny morning, as Misti planned to skip the biology practical class but she had to attend as Ravi forced her and promised to help her with the practical. Misti hated practical classes, as it's not really ideal thing to cut a frog or dissect a cockroach. While, Manjula was an over enthusiastic kid, who always dreamt to bring a revolutionary change in the whole molecular set up of our body. Human body intrigues her. She was having a little trouble understanding the digestive system, so she asked the teacher for an explanation of the system. Rajiv Desai asked her to meet him at his chamber after class. She was innocent enough to catch his intentions early. So she went there as the class ended. When he shifted his discussion from digestive to reproduction system to male parts she was alarmed. She did not waste a minute to ring an alarm on the incident. As a result of which the entire plan was chalked.

The first action plan was to execute a secret signature campaign with all the students of the Dehradun boarding school. This was followed by the final action plan execution under the sole command of our own Misti i.e., Mridula Ghosh. The day started with the formal prayers at the auditorium of the school. Misti was about to sing the prayers after being called up by the principal Malhotra. Misti stood there in front of the mike and she took hold of it. Instead of prayers she sang a self-composed poem. The poem was a mockery to the school authority with the charge of neglect and inefficiency towards the wellbeing of the students. The principal instantly grabbed the mike, "What are you singing Mridula?"

She just smiled at him and Ravi made the first gesture by clapping to it. Then the entire audience of the auditorium clapped. They broke out - 'Save Davidson Boarding, Save Dehradun School'.

Principal asked everyone to stop but the buzz grew to an unbearable level. There were threats of gherao[37]. The principal handled the crisis situation by promising to take action against the Biology Teacher, after the trustee meeting. Till then everyone must resume class.

That evening the trustee meeting was called and so was the buzz creator Misti. One member said that this happened first and the last time in two decades, "Immediately we owe an explanation from her. Why did she take such stern step that blew out of proportion? Instead she could have complained to the Principal or written to the higher authorities." Another member said, "What you want to be a leader or what?" Then another added, "You know we can even expel you? Don't you have any fear?"

She said, "What fear in standing for justice? Here is the signature of all the students in my favor. Now it's your choice- me or that pervert."

Principal exclaimed, "Oh, please stop. You may go now."

---

[37]   Circle the person preventing any mobility

The next four hours were an anxious wait for students. Finally the academics offered a middle path. They will not expel anyone that would harm the reputation of the school. But the biology teacher will apologize in public for his deeds. The crowd burst in anger, and they shouted out which finally lead to a gherao of about 24hours. Then finally the decision was made to bid final blow to the Biology Teacher.

With the decision Misti soon became the hero of the school. They celebrated the victory with various songs like- chale chalo of film Lagaan.

16

CRACK IN THE HEAVEN

The day which had started with great surprise from Mohan was going as quite disturbing with one upsetting reality i.e., *he* is still single. I was having strange doubts- it could be for me that Arvind had waited all along. It was in that tormenting moment that tears streaked down my cheek. But with a sudden jolt as the bird's call (ringing of the calling bell) I realized it was quite late. I immediately rubbed off the tears and rushed to get the door. It could be Mohan, I thought. And indeed it was him.

Mohan asked, "What took you so long to open honey?"

"I was in the kitchen."

"Don't tell me you were preparing something special for me."

I did not reply to that and smiled, "I was just making the usual lunch shona."

Mohan taking off his boots extended his hand towards me, "Come close, sit here, I have big news to share."

"Okay."

"As you must know Mr. Bose and I were contending for the same position in our head quarter in London. It had almost been a huddle race to reach the target. Finally I won; yes our London dreams are coming true. And we are shifting by next month, what say?"

I was completely at awe, "Our London dreams? What are you saying? Misti is admitted at one of the finest school in India. I have my work and book coming up. You just had a promotion and now you are talking of shifting our base, impossible, impossible, and impossible."

"I knew you would make big deal about it. You never support me and my decisions."

"You mean your irrational decisions."

"Stop it please. Okay I will drop the offer, are you happy now?"

I showed doubts on this compromise formula, mocked at him saying, "Make a legitimate choice, if you think it's good for you, then take it. Only I and my daughter are not coming."

"Enough of this argument, I don't want to talk with you."

Mohan whose dreams were suddenly crushed had no clue what the real reason behind Lathika's harsh behavior. On the other hand, Lathika was not in herself. Something went very wrong, something has changed. She doesn't seem to be the same woman who hugged and kissed him and felt blessed at this happy married life. At that moment silence prevailed in the house till Lathika served the delicious food for that afternoon. Still there was no talking at the table. When the phone rang it sounded like an alarming horn in the room.

Mohan took the phone, "Hello!"

"Is it Mr. Mohan Ghosh?"

Mohan asked, "Yes, who is it?"

I thought the call might be from some insurance agent or bank or kitchen chimney seller or solar energy cooking medium seller. This was quite obvious for me to think as most of the days they call up at this hour. Their targets are the housewives who are easily lured to try and buy things. But today was an exception.

Mohan came out worried, "Lathiii…"

"What happened?" I sensed his worries, "Is Misti alright?"

"Her Principal wants to meet us."

"Why? Is she not good with grades?"

"Her grades are fine. Actually she wrote a poem."

Mohan took off for the day and while I booked flight tickets on the net. Someone just pumped back blood into their relation which was going dead a while ago.

When we reached there, it was quite late yet the Principal agreed to meet them as it was very urgent. We were informed about the entire incident that took place in the campus. The Principal particularly pointed out the capacity of a girl of her age to organize such an event single handedly. This is something to be admired yet could be dangerous if not controlled. But they cannot take any action against her, because she was right to a point. So he felt the parents should know what their child was up to and decide whether she would continue there.

Misti came back. She was to stay at home for some time and if she realized her mistake she would be allowed to rejoin the school or she would have to be admitted to the same school where Aryan Bose studied.

Misti who did not oppose her father's decision to bring her back, finally broke her silence as her mother brought up the issue of Aryan's school, "No way Mom, I am not going to that school. I am innocent and I feel like vindicated. Ravi was right, unlike his parents; mine will never support but make me suffer."

I asked, "Who is Ravi now? Your *gyan guru*[38]?"

Misti screamed, "NO, MY BOYFRIEND!"
I slapped Misti and she cried, "I hate you Mom."
"That's okay."
Mohan,"Ufff... Lathi you are incorrigible."
Misti went on a fast. Finally Misti's fasting broke with hot Knorr Soup and kisses on both her cheeks from her parents.

Days passed, yet another afternoon, a call startled me, "Oh Arvind this is not the right time ....please some other time....oh it's urgent, then hold on a second please."

I sneaked out of my room, checked Misti reading something in her room and came back with silent steps. I slide my door and spoke softly, "Tell me Arvind."

---

[38]   One who advices

"I am coming to Bengaluru for a day or two; I would be staying in The Park Hotel. I request you to come and visit at least for once. Please."

"Oh dear! But I can't." I sob.

Arvind exclaimed, "Why, why, why? It seems even after all these years you haven't forgiven me, okay forget it. Let me die with all the burdens on my shoulder, let my wounds linger; at least you will be happy."

"Don't speak like that I will come, I will."

"Promise?"

"Promise."

That night I could not close my eyes a bit. I stayed awake thinking what possibly could happen. There was a hidden fear in the chamber of my heart. But could say what is the fear is hard to tell because I have long gone over my feelings for Arvind and I overtly claim to be happily married with Mohan.

I still could not make up my mind if I want to meet Arvind at The Park Hotel. Though next day I gathered courage to go out of home in the afternoon, saying I had to go to the office to personally submit some papers. I was playing a great gamble with my life doing this. I knew this at the back of my mind but I must not disappoint Arvind as he too had suffered a lot. It was sympathy mixed with curiosity that led me to the hotel at last.

Arvind was already waiting at the lobby area before I arrived. His heart stopped at the sight of his love. Arvind's life has not changed a bit since the hospital incident. As if he stood still for ages waiting for me. Not a leaf had fallen, not a page had turned, no breath was taken, that moment and this moment that merged into one.

At first I brood as what to say and what not. I didn't have a clue how to start. When Arvind spoke as gently he walked towards- "Hello, Lathi, I knew you would come."

"I had to, didn't I?"

"So you did forgive me."

I felt hesitant to answer rather to continue conversation with public vigilance especially when Arvind is a public figure, "Let's go someplace maybe a cafeteria where we can talk like two normal adult people without public glare."

"Come to my room. I mean only if you feel comfortable."

I nodded in affirmation and we walked through the long decorated hallway to his room. The room was also decorated with new touch in everything, "Flawless perfection!"

Arvind says, "Flawless forever you mean."

"I meant the room."

"I meant you."

"Stop it. I know I am a grown woman of forties and lack the charm I once had."

"To me you are the same."

"It is because…"

"Because?"

I bit my lower lip in hesitation, "I don't know."

"Because I madly love you. Yes it's true which you clearly don't believe."

"I believe you. I believed you even when you left at the hotel room unalarmed and I believe even now."

"Can you please don't bring up the mishap in our conversation?"

"It's just not a mishap for me. It changed my life forever."

"It changed for good isn't it?"

"Oh yes, Mohan loves me like anything."

"Ah! I see..."

He had turned his face to the wall. He pressed his upper lip against another as he felt like crying.

"Oh Arvind, don't cry....why didn't you try to contact me then?"

"Because I had promised your parents."

"Then why now?"

"Because I thought fourteen years of separation was enough. Now is the time or never."

I hugged him tight in his arms and we cried together for the last time. Then after a little this and that, I watched that the time was pretty late.

I was in haste but I promised to keep in touch over mails and calls.

Arvind said, "Come let me get you a cab."

And as we walked along the gate, suddenly out of no-where a bunch of journalist gathered around us. Arvind hauled me but failed to stop the press in taking pictures and videos.

"What's going on Arvind?"

"I have no idea."

I pushed through the crowded gate and took a cab, "Bhaiya take me to Koramangala."

I then turned around and found Arvind still standing there looking helpless with fear of being misunderstood once again.

My phone biped, I checked it to find Mohan's sms flashing on the screen- 'where are you? I am worried?'

I saw the message but could not reply to it. And then the wind roared and rain poured heavily in symmetry with my tears. The cab driver watched me through the rear view mirror and he too had few lectures for me, "Ma'am, these are the complexities of urban life, no one leaves you alone and there is nothing called privacy."

I reached my destination still very tired with the disturbing words of wisdom from the cab driver. When I knocked Mohan opened immediately. Before they could speak Misti cried out, "Look Mom you are in TV."

Mohan had turned his back to the dining table holding his mobile in his left ear, "Oh no Mrs. Bose, they are just acquaintances...the media is just framing the issue... you want to talk to her...but she is just too tired...yes of course...okay thank you, bye."

I sat on the couch with calm composure. My silent reaction was not enough to pacify the unwarranted worries of my darling hubby. Mohan said, "It's okay dear I am in charge of everything. You don't worry. By the way how do you know him?"

"We were in university together."

"And you had quite intimacy with him, right?"

"No we were just classmates."

"Oh so you went to meet him knowing he is in here. Well that explains it all. As I said earlier, no worries, okay?"

I knew that there are a thousand reasons to be worried now and I resort to my calmness in handling the situation. I walked towards my room and from the corner of my eyes I could guess both father and daughter were worried big time. I realized that time has come that Mohan should stand face to face with the reality. But for now I must maintain my silence.

That night after tugging off Misti to bed, I walked towards my bedroom with hesitant steps. Mohan was engrossed in reading Chetan Bhagat's latest book.

"I have something to tell you, rather a confession," I mumbled.

Mohan, the chatterbox kept his patience initially. Then he thundered, "You whore, how twisted the reality in your favor all along and now you went out to have sex with your ex?"

"I have not done anything wrong Mohan. You have to believe me."

"Believe you after all this? You must think me a big fool."

I stood at the corner of the bed and tried to justify, "No dear no, you are my only support in this entire world."

Mohan felt like a loser, but he promised to stay by my side through all the coming turmoil. But as soon as everything came to normal, he would file a divorce. He added, "And I want my daughter to live with me and not you."

"You cannot have her, because she is not yours."

"What do you mean?"

"You are not her real father Mohan."

Mohan left the room that night with his pillow and then left the apartment the next day. When he turned his face was firm with a decision never to return to this house, for the last time he peeped through the door of the dark chamber of his beloved daughter Misti and left for lifetime.

17

TO THE NEW BEGINNING

$\mathcal{D}$ad had called next morning when the turmoil reached its peak, "What had happened Lathi? The national media stated that you had been spotted with Minister Arvind. They have published photos and even covered the news in television. What's going on, tell me dear."

I broke down, "Dad, Mohan left home in anger, I am afraid as he was very upset."

"Why, what have you told him?"

"I told him everything, told him the link up was not crafted rather was reality. I also told him that Misti is not his daughter."

"Are you out of your mind? What have you done? You could have consulted me before taking such action."

"I did try to call you Dad but…"

"It's okay dear, don't worry. Nothing happens overnight; let him melt down a bit and then he will come in his senses."

"Okay Dad."

I disconnected the phone on a positive note but feeling helpless. I stood there as the captain of a stranded ship. Misti woke up by the commotion of constant phone ringing, "What's going on Mom? Where is Dad? Why are you so worried?"

I decided to confess, "Your father has left us shona."

"Why are you saying so Maa?"

"He is mad at me dear."

"You must be wrong, okay let me try his number."

I did not stop her from calling him. But he did not pick. Then there was another call on the land number. Both of them rushed to the bed room.

I picked up, "Oh Mrs. Bose…"

"So you are quite famous now."

"C'mon Mrs. Bose."

"Ha ha just kidding. Come let's go out for shopping at the Inorbit mall. They are offering flat forty percent off only for today."

"I can't. Mohan is out in anger."

"Oh don't worry he will come back. Raghav always says he has never seen a docile husband as Mohan."

"Please spare me for today. I will surely catch up with you later."

I hung up. Yet another call and another call and another came. Everyone but Mohan called. Once Arvind had called which Lathi listened quietly without any protest, "I am going back to Kolkata. I know I have done real damage to your reputation by asking you to meet me but believe me I had no idea about the press."

"Hmm…"

I had no words to console him while my own wounds were left open. Days passed waiting for Mohan and his call. Misti cried and cried, "When will he be back, Mom?"

She kept asking the same question. And repeatedly I replied, "He will, he soon will."

My concern over Misti grew as she had fever over 104 degree centigrade for the last four days. I must do something I told myself. So I straight went to his office and walked down his chamber, "This has to stop. Don't you have any responsibility towards your family?"

I avoided any eye contact and continued, "Your daughter is ill and she is in this condition because of you."

Mohan busted in anger, "Because of me, who am I to her?"

"C'mon Mohan you are everything, you are her father."

"Then why did you tell me the other day?"

"I am so sorry Mohan. Come now don't make a scene here."

Mohan had come back. He had been staying at a hotel for couple of days during his anger session. Now after reaching home he took a fresh bath.

Misti, Mohan and I are having a pillow fight once again as if nothing had happened. But something did happen. In the inner depth of my soul I mourn at the thought that someday Misti will surely learn that Arvind Singh, the 'Man of Disaster' as she called him, was her real father.

But who cares about the future. We are busy now packing for England, as Mohan did accepted the offer from office. This time I did approve. Finally, Misti sets the camera and a selfie was taken to be sent to Ravi, the ex-army man's son whose life and love is Misti. Aryan Bose still desires for this young vivacious girl in his life. This is yet another story to be told again some other time. Till then let's enjoy the moment with a cup of coffee.

Epilogue

Love is something that enriches to life the most, something without which you cannot live. It changes your habits for good. You become more sincere and matured about your loved ones.

Lathika's life went through scanner and she passed out with flying colors fighting all odds. But five years down the line things will not be the same. Soon Misti will come to know about her real father and will leave house to meet the man. Arvind will become the key man in state politics. With more responsibilities on his shoulder will he entertain Misti in his life? Lathi with her troublesome daughter will have to fight for her peace once again.

That's life. Which seems complicated at times and this complication is all because of love. Love binds and even parts lives. What is hold in the future is something to be contemplated. A single step of Misti will bring revolution in the Ghosh household. Or she chooses to keep her mouth shut in front of the father whom she had never met before. Whatever she does will change the lives forever.

The perception of love will completely change for readers when we go ahead with the story in the next series. It's Lathika's life and she cannot let anything happen to it. She can do anything to make it right. What is there for us is something we need to wait for reading in the coming days.

Printed in the United States
By Bookmasters